DISCARD

PIGGLE

PIGGLE

An I CAN READ Book

by Crosby Bonsall

Harper & Row, Publishers
New York, Evanston, San Francisco, London

*for H. L. S., the Duchess
with love*

"We don't want
to play with you,"
said Lolly, Molly, Polly and Dolly.
They were Homer's sisters.
"We are playing a game.
We are playing Pin the Tail,
and we don't need you."

"Beans," said Homer.

He went to see Duck.

"Will you play a game with me?"

Homer asked Duck.

"What game?" Duck asked.

"Anything," Homer said.

Duck said, "I don't know

that game."

And he swam away.

"Beans," said Homer.

He went to see Rabbit.

"Will you play a game with me?"

Homer asked Rabbit.

"What are you playing?"

Rabbit asked.

"Nothing, yet," Homer said.

"Well then," said Rabbit,

"you don't need me to play that."

And he hopped away.

"Beans," said Homer.

He went to see Pig.

"Hello, Pig," Homer said.

"Will you play a game with me?"

"What game?" Pig asked.

"I don't care," Homer said.

"Never heard of that game,"
said Pig.

"What game?" Homer asked.

"I Don't Care," said Pig.

"That is not a game," Homer said.

"Then why did you ask me
to play?" asked Pig.

"I asked you to play SOMETHING,"
Homer said.

"I don't know that game either,"
Pig said.

"Aw, beans," said Homer.

"Look, Pig," Homer said,

"do *you* know a game to play?"

Pig thought for a while.

"Maybe," he said.

"Well, do you or don't you?"

Homer asked.

"I might," said Pig.

"Yes, or no?" Homer said.

"Mmmmmm," said Pig.

"What does that mean?" Homer asked.

Pig said, "It means

I am thinking."

"Well, don't take so long,"

Homer said.

"Mmmmmm," said Pig.

"You don't know a game,"

Homer cried.

"I do too know a game," Pig said. "I will think of it in a minute."

Homer waited . . . and waited.

"Hurry up, Pig," he said.

"I am getting tired."

"I know a game!" Pig cried.

"The game is Piggle.

It is the best game

in the whole world.

It is the most fun

of anything.

It is named after me,

and I play it all the time.

So there!"

"Okay," said Homer. "Let's play."

"I don't want to," said Pig.

"Beans," said Homer. "Beans,
beans, beans, beans, BEANS!"

Homer sat down to think,

and he fell asleep. . . .

"Let's play Pin the Tail

on Rabbit,"

cried Lolly, Molly, Polly and Dolly.

"What a dumb thing," Rabbit said.

"I have a tail.

I don't need another tail.

And nobody is going to

STICK A PIN IN ME!"

"It's only a game,"

said Lolly and Molly.

"Let's play Pin the Tail on Pig,"

said Polly and Dolly.

"I have a tail," Pig cried.

"I don't need another tail.

And nobody is going to

STICK A PIN IN ME!"

"You're no fun,"

said Lolly and Molly.

"Let's play Pin the Tail on Duck,"

said Polly and Dolly.

Duck said, "I have a tail.

I don't need another tail.

And nobody is going to

STICK A PIN IN ME!"

"You must find someone

who needs a tail," Rabbit said.

"Or pin a tail on one of you,"

said Pig.

28

"Oh, no," cried Lolly, Molly, Polly and Dolly.

"That's no fun.

But we know someone.

We will pin a tail on him."

And Lolly,

Molly,

Polly

and Dolly

looked . . .

right . . .

at . . .

Homer.

"I don't want a tail,"

Homer cried.

"I don't want to play.

I don't like this game."

"What a silly thing," Pig said.

"He wanted to play before,

and now he doesn't want to."

"What a pest," said Duck.

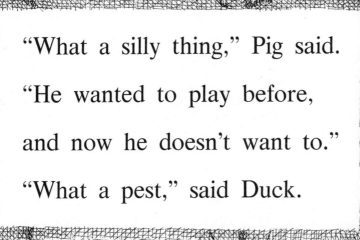

"Just like Homer," snapped Rabbit.

"Hot and cold, off and on,

in and out. He can't

make up his mind."

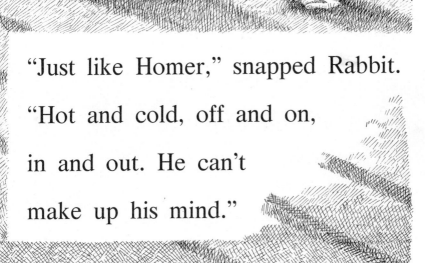

"Beans," Homer said.

"I *can* make up my mind.

I don't want to play.

I want to go home."

"Not without a tail," Pig said.

"Just hold still," Duck said.

"It will only

take a minute," Rabbit said.

"And it won't hurt a bit,"

cried Lolly, Molly,

Polly and Dolly.

"I don't want a tail!"

yelled Homer.

"I DON'T WANT A TAIL!

I DON'T WANT A TAIL!"

"I DON'T WANT A TAIL!"

Homer yelled again. . . .

"Well, if you don't want a tail,"

Bear said,

"you don't have to have one."

"Hello, Bear," Homer said.

"I am *so* glad to see you.

They want to pin a tail on me."

"They don't really," Bear said.

"You were dreaming.

But it's all right now.

You're awake and I am here."

"Oh, Bear, thank you," Homer said.

"Will you play a game with me?"

Bear said, "Yes, I will.

What shall we play?"

"Do you know a game

called Piggle?" Homer asked.

"Piggle . . . Piggle," Bear said.

"Piggle like triggle, hmmmm."

"Triggle, Bear?" Homer said.

"Triggle," Bear said.

"Triggle like biggle."

"Oh," said Homer.

"Let me think," said Bear.

"Piggle like miggle."

"Miggle, Bear?" Homer said.

"Miggle like diggle," Bear said.

"Oh," said Homer.

"Give me time," said Bear.

"Let me see now, we have

triggle and biggle,

miggle and diggle like Piggle."

"Oh, *I* see," cried Homer.

"Let me try.

Wiggle, giggle,

sniggle and figgle like Piggle.

That's *it*, Bear. I can play!"

"Yes, you can," cried Bear.

"Maybe I know the game of Piggle after all. It sounds nice."

"Yes, it does," Homer said.

"Let's piggle some more.

Ishy, wishy, fishy, dishy."

Bear sang, "Diddley, widdley, fiddley, riddley."

And together they sang,

"Mumpity, wumpity, dumpity, lumpity."

"What are you playing?"

asked Lolly, Molly, Polly and Dolly.

"Piggle," cried Homer.

"What is Piggle?"

asked Lolly, Molly, Polly and Dolly.

"This is Piggle," said Homer—

"hinkity, pinkity, dinkity, winkity."

"What are you playing?"
asked Rabbit and Duck.
"Piggle," cried Homer.

"What is that?"

asked Rabbit and Duck.

"This is Piggle," Homer said.

And he sang, "Willagin, millagin,

pillagin, gillagin."

"Hey, what are you playing?"

Pig asked.

"Don't you know?" Homer said.

"No," said Pig.

Homer said, "Oh, Pig,

don't you know

the best game

in the whole world?

Don't you know the game

that is the most fun

of anything?

Don't you know the game

named after you

that you play

ALL THE TIME?

Don't you know Piggle?"

"Oh," said Pig,

"is *that* Piggle?

How do you play?"

"Like this," said Lolly,

Molly, Polly and Dolly.

And they sang,

"Lolly, Molly, Polly, Dolly."

"No, like this," yelled Duck.

"Tacky, dacky, wacky, quacky."

"No," shouted Rabbit, "like this.

Sunny, runny, funny, bunny."

"I get it!" said Pig. And he sang,

"Plump, clever, rosy,

sweet, clean Pig."

"Wrong, wrong, wrong, wrong!"
yelled Lolly, Molly,
Polly and Dolly.
"You don't know how to play Piggle!"
shouted Duck and Rabbit.

"I do too know how to play Piggle,"

Pig said. "After all, it's *my* game."

And Pig slapped Duck.

And Duck bit Rabbit.

And Rabbit kicked Lolly.

And Lolly pinched Molly.

And Molly punched Polly.

And Polly pushed Dolly.

"Beans," said Homer.

"Who wants to play
with them, anyway?"

"I don't," said Bear.

"Then let's go," said Homer,
"far away."

"Where it is quiet," said Bear.

And they ran off to find

a quiet place . . .

and they almost did.